ED & DAVE

I went to the party in
Kalamazoo

Written by
Ed Shankman

Illustrated by
Dave Frank

Copyright © 2001 by Ed Shankman and Dave Frank

Published in the United States by Two Kids Productions, LLC
Printed in Singapore
ISBN 0-615-12092-X

2 4 6 8 10 9 7 5 3

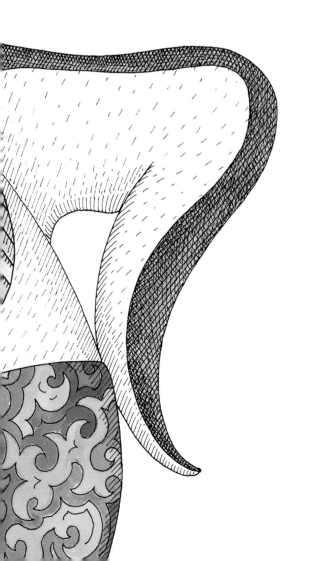

Ten years from today
wherever you are,
put on your best clothes
and climb into your car.

Then drive out to meet us
and bring your friends too,
'cause we're having a party
in Kalamazoo.

You won't want to miss it.
You simply must go.
And you must invite
all of the people you know.

And I'll invite my friends
and they'll invite theirs,
and they may come alone,
or they could come in pairs.

They'll come from Geneva,
New York and St. Paul.
And some won't have too far
to travel at all.

And everyone *they* know
will want to come too,
and they'll all join the party
in Kalamazoo.

We'll get there by train
and we'll get there by plane.
And one guy will walk
the whole way with a cane.

We'll come in the morning.
We'll come by canoe.
And we'll all be together
in Kalamazoo.

You'll meet Never-Sleep Norman
who won't go to bed,
a very tall man
with a very small head,
three skinny catfish
who laugh when they dance,
and a ten-legged fellow
with five pairs of pants.

You'll meet bunnies and billy goats,
bears and baboons,
'cause everyone's coming
and they're bringing balloons!

And some will bring cookies,
and some will bring cake,
or whatever they buy,
or whatever they make.

One might bring a tuba.
One could bring a drum.
One may bring a bell
that he rings with his thumb.

If I bring the jelly,
you might bring the toast,
or whatever the thing is
that *you* like the most.

Whatever it is, we will gladly allow.
And you can be sure
we will use it somehow.

'Cause there must be
ten million ways to have fun,
and in Kalamazoo
we will try every one!

I don't know you well
but you look like a smarty.
I'm sure you'll have
lots of ideas for the party.

We can sing till we're hoarse.
We can eat till we're fat.
We can stay up all night
or much later than that.

There'll be sandboxes everywhere
and fields to play ball in …

and places to hide in
and places to crawl in
and places to lie in
and others to fall in …

... and one place I'm sure
you will feel very tall in.

Yes indeed, what a party
that party will be —
every part of that party
will be something to see.

There'll be puppies and ponies
and marionettes.
That's the kind of excitement
that *no one* forgets!

We can swim.
We can hike.
We can ride on a bike.
We can yell if we want to
whenever we like.

We can climb on the ceiling
and paint on the wall.
We can bounce on the beds.
We can run in the hall.

Want to make funny faces?
Go ahead, have a ball.
We'll see who makes
the funniest faces of all!

We'll pretend that we're lizards
and lobsters and loons.
And then, if you like,
we can watch some cartoons.

We can do as we please
'cause the party is ours.
We don't have to behave.
We don't have to take showers.

If you want to do nothing,
that's just what we'll do.
We'll do nothing together
in Kalamazoo.

And then, in the end,
when we've had all our fun,
when the last joke is told
and the last game is done …

we'll say our goodbyes
and we'll all go back home,
to our homes in Ohio
and Brooklyn and Rome.

We'll go back to our homes
for the rest of our days,
to our regular lives
and our usual ways.

But forever and ever,
wherever you go,
whoever you meet
will be eager to know ...